P9-EED-974

This book belongs to

_____

_____

tiger tales
an imprint of ME Media, LLC
202 Old Ridgefield Road, Wilton, CT 06897
Published in the United States 2008
Originally published in Great Britain 2008
by Little Tiger Press
an imprint of Magi Publications
Text copyright © 2008 Paul Bright
Illustrations copyright © 2008 Ruth Galloway
CIP data is available
ISBN-13: 978-1-58925-409-1
ISBN-10: 1-58925-409-0
Printed in China
All rights reserved
1 3 5 7 9 10 8 6 4 2

Fidgety Fish
and Friends

by Paul Bright

Illustrated by Ruth Galloway

tiger tales

swoosh!

FIDGETY FISH
I love to flip and fidget,
To dive and dart and dash.
I wiggle my bottom and jiggle my tail,
With a fidgety swish, splish, splash!

SMILEY SHARK

All sensible sharks agree,
I'm as silly as a shark can be.
I giggle and grin if you tickle my fin,
And wriggle my tail with glee.

AMAZING ANGELFISH

There are short fish, long fish, thin fish, fat fish,

Funny-looking flat fish, dogfish, catfish.

Some are very big, some are teeny-weeny small.

Can I be the one who is the prettiest of all?

CLICKETY CRAB

My snip-snap claws go clickety-click,
My legs tap a tune on the sand.
I sing and I drum, and I whistle and hum,
I'm the wonderful one-crab band!

SHY OCTOPUS

Octopus hides inside his cave,
He's really very shy.
So please give him a friendly wave,
Next time you're passing by.

JIGGLY JELLYFISH
We wibble and we wobble,
Like jelly in a dish.

WHOOSH!

SPECTACULAR STARFISH

We're the spectacular starfish,

We swirl and we twirl all about.

We skip and we spin as the tide's coming in,

Then again as the tide's going out.

SHINY SNAILS

Ten little sea snails,
Hiding in the sea.
Each has a bright shell,
Shiny as can be.

SUPER SEA HORSES

Can you see the sea horses? Can you spot a snout?

Can you find a tail or a tummy sticking out?

Can you see the sea horse friends, all playing peekaboo?

Jumping out and laughing, shouting, "I've found you!"

PROUD PUFFER FISH

Why does a puffer fish puff, puff, puff!

Only the puffer fish knows.

He blows out his chest with a huff, huff, huff!

And grows and grows and grows!

TERRIFIC TURTLE

See the fish join in the fun
When Turtle comes to play.
Chasing, hiding, swooshing, gliding,
Laughing all the way.

FIDGETY FISH AND FRIENDS

Swimming and skittering under the sea,
With a smile and a swirl and a swish.
All of his friends love to play every day
With the fabulous Fidgety Fish!

Dinosaurs Galore!
by Giles Andreae
Illustrated by David Wojtowycz
ISBN-13: 978-1-58925-399-5
ISBN-10: 1-58925-399-X

The Witch with a Twitch
by Layn Marlow
Illustrated by Joelle Dreidemy
ISBN-13: 978-1-58925-400-8
ISBN-10: 1-58925-400-7

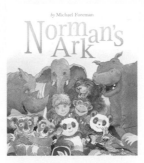

Norman's Ark
by Michael Foreman
ISBN-13: 978-1-58925-401-5
ISBN-10: 1-58925-401-5

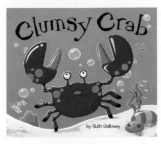

Clumsy Crab
by Ruth Galloway
ISBN-13: 978-1-58925-402-2
ISBN-10: 1-58925-402-3

Explore the world of tiger tales!

More fun-filled and exciting stories await you!
Look for these titles and more
at your local library or bookstore.
And have fun reading!

tiger tales
202 Old Ridgefield Road, Wilton, CT 06897

The Crunching Munching Caterpillar
by Sheridan Cain
Illustrated by Jack Tickle
ISBN-13: 978-1-58925-403-9
ISBN-10: 1-58925-403-1

The Very Ugly Bug
by Liz Pichon
ISBN-13: 978-1-58925-404-6
ISBN-10: 1-58925-404-X

Good Night, Sleep Tight!
by Claire Freedman
Illustrated by Rory Tyger
ISBN-13: 978-1-58925-405-3
ISBN-10: 1-58925-405-8

Hound Dog
by David Bedford
Illustrated by Melanie Williamson
ISBN-13: 978-1-58925-397-1
ISBN-10: 1-58925-397-3